Boots Goes to School

Written by
Sara James

Illustrated by
Pamiel Barcita

SMITHMARK

Kidsbooks Inc.
7004 N. California Avenue
Chicago, IL 60645

This edition published in 1993 by SMITHMARK Publishers Inc.,
16 East 32nd Street, New York, NY 10016.

SMITHMARK books are available for bulk purchase
for sales promotion and premium use.
For details, write or telephone the Manager of Special Sales,
SMITHMARK Publishers Inc., 16 East 32nd Street,
New York, NY 10016. (212) 532-6600

Manufactured in the United States of America

"Hi, everyone," said Boots. "Are you ready for school?"

"You bet," said Doogie Bowser, "and I have a brand new lunchbox."

"I have a new notebook," said Rita Rabbit.
"I have four sharp pencils," said Buddy Bear.
"I have a new ball for recess," said Gina Giraffe.
"And I have a box of crayons," said Boots.

"Good morning, class," said Ms. Appleby.
"I am your new teacher."

"We're going to have a great time today. But first I would like you to raise your hand when I call your name so I know that you are here."

When Ms. Appleby was through taking attendance, she asked the class if they would like to paint some pictures.

"Yes!" shouted everyone as they put on smocks and helped set up the easels.

Boots drew a picture of his family.
Gina painted a tall, tall tree.

Buddy Bear drew a big bowl of honey and Rita
Rabbit painted a picture of herself.

Next, it was storytime.

"Once upon a time," began Ms. Appleby as she read her favorite fairy tale, *Goldilocks and the Three Bears.*

Everyone knew the story, but it was great fun hearing Ms. Appleby read it.

When Ms. Appleby was through, Boots felt a rumble in his tummy. "It must be time for lunch," he thought.

Sure enough, Boots heard the lunch bell and followed everyone out to the lunchroom.

"What do you have in your new lunchbox, Doogie?" asked Boots.

"A peanut butter and jelly sandwich with apple juice and graham crackers."

"I've got tuna fish, grape juice, and two apples," said Boots.

"Why two apples?" asked Rita.

"It's a surprise," said Boots.

After lunch Ms. Appleby took out the musical instruments.

"We're going to form a class band, and everyone is going to have a part to play," she said.

Boots got the triangle. It went *ding* when he struck it.

Gina played the cymbals which *clanged* together.

Buddy pounded the drum, *bum, bum, bum*.

After, the entire class gathered around the piano. Ms. Appleby played and everyone sang rounds of *Row, Row, Row Your Boat* until they couldn't sing anymore.

"It's snack time. Who wants to help me?"
asked Ms. Appleby after all the instruments
were put away.

"I do, I do," shouted Boots.

Boots handed out all the cups as Ms. Appleby filled them with juice. Then Boots gave every student two chocolate chip cookies.

"Would you also like two cookies?" Boots asked his teacher.

"No thanks, Boots. I know it's hard to believe, but I don't really like cookies," answered Ms. Appleby.

"Then I have the perfect snack for you," said Boots.

"You do?" she replied.

"Yes. Here's an apple. Teachers always like apples." said Boots.

"Why thank you, Boots. What a nice surprise," said Ms. Appleby as she took a big bite!